Town Mouse and Country Mouse

Belling the Cat

The Dog and the Wolf

THREE FABLES FROM AESOP

retold by Cynthia Swain

Table of Contents

FABLES

What is a fable?

A fable (FAY-bul) is a very short story. All fables teach a lesson, or moral (MOR-ul). In most fables, the characters are animals.

What is the purpose of a fable?

Fables teach people lessons. Fables point out foibles (FOY-bulz) that people have. A foible is a character flaw. Being boastful is a flaw. Being dishonest is also a flaw. Fables show why the flaw is bad. Fables are also fun to read. Most of us enjoy poking fun at one another.

Who invented fables?

People have told fables for thousands of years. Ancient peoples around the world all told fables. Later, in the Middle Ages, people continued this way of storytelling. Today, some authors still use the fable genre.

How do you read a fable?

When you read a fable, note the title. The title will tell you who the main characters are. Each character stands for ways that humans behave. Ask yourself, *What human trait does each character show?* Then note what happens to the main characters. Think about how the events teach the moral.

Features of a Fable

The main characters are usually animals.

The story is brief.

At least one character has a flaw or problem.

The story has a moral stated at the end.

One character learns something from another character.

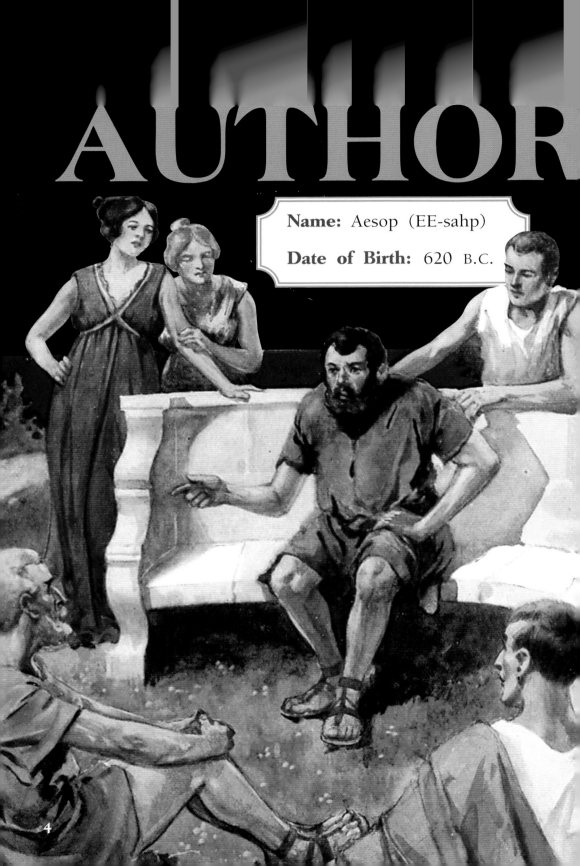

AUTHOR

Name: Aesop (EE-sahp)

Date of Birth: 620 B.C.

Place of Birth: No one is sure where Aesop was born. Many places in Greece and Africa have claimed to be his birthplace.

His Life: Most people who study history think Aesop was born a slave. While a slave, he lived on the Greek island of Samos (SAY-mahs). Later, he was given his freedom and became active in public affairs. Aesop traveled through many countries and met with great thinkers and rulers. While employed by the ruler Croesus (KREE-sus), he visited many cities and shared fables to help bring the people together under Croesus's rule.

His Works: Most people agree that Aesop never wrote down his fables himself. Around 300 B.C., a Greek philosopher, Phalereus (fuh-LAIR-ee-us), made the first collection of Aesop's fables.

Tools Writers Use
Idiom

An **idiom** (IH-dee-um) is a phrase or expression that makes language more colorful and interesting. Idioms do not use the literal (exact) meaning of the phrase. Consider the sentence: "Ken is such a penny-pincher that he won't buy an umbrella to keep off the rain." This does not mean that Ken actually squeezes coins. Instead, it means that Ken does not like to spend money. Since idioms are commonly used in conversation and writing, people grow to understand what they mean in a particular culture.

Town Mouse and Country Mouse

Town Mouse and Country Mouse were cousins. They spent summers together growing up. They were good friends. They were thick as thieves. They were still very close. But they had very different opinions. They came from very different places. They had different thoughts. They had different ideas. They had different points of view. The mouse cousins could never agree on anything.

"The country is **superior** to the town," said Country Mouse. "Come over, Cousin. I'll show you that it is better."

Town Mouse agreed to go, but he was **determined** to show Country Mouse a thing or two. He would show that the town was the best place.

Town Mouse went to Country Mouse's farm. Country Mouse had been working day and night. It was harvest time. He was putting corn into the barn. He was putting wheat into the barn.

"Country Mouse," said Town Mouse. "You work like a dog. Why do you bother?"

"I need to have food for winter," said Country Mouse. "Look how much I have to eat all year long. This is why the country is best. Don't you agree?"

"Hold your horses, Cousin!" said Town Mouse. "Let me taste this corn. Then I will answer."

"Well?" said Country Mouse after a while. "Tell the truth, Town Mouse. What do you think about the country?"

"You do have lots of food," Town Mouse said. "But it's not as tasty as the food in town. My food will knock your socks off! Visit me. I will prove how good it is."

A few weeks passed. Country Mouse went to town. He stayed with his cousin. The cousins went to the basement. They went to a garbage can there.

"At night, people leave this food," said Town Mouse. "I don't have to work for my food like you do. Look—there's pizza. Yum! It has extra cheese. There's cake! There's ice cream!"

The two cousins jumped into the can. The food was fit for a king. It was tasty. Country Mouse ate everything. "You were right!" said Country Mouse. "That was **delectable**." Country Mouse's little belly was full. He was on cloud nine!

Town Mouse was very happy. His cousin would have to face the facts. The town was better than the country.

"Say it, Cousin," said Town Mouse. "The town is better than the country."

Suddenly there was a loud noise. Country Mouse was scared. "What is that?" he asked. He was shaking with fear.

"Why, you're afraid of your own shadow. Don't be so **squeamish**!" said Town Mouse. "In the town, there are many scary noises. They sound bad. But do not worry."

9

The sound grew closer. The sound grew louder. Country Mouse's heart beat quickly. "I may be from the country, but that's not just a noise. That's a cat!"

"Yes, it is a cat. Every night, the cat tries to catch me. Every night, I run away. It's fun! Don't you think that's fun?"

Country Mouse did not like that game. "I'm hitting the road," he said. He ran out from the garbage can. He ran fast. He ran all the way home. The town had a lot of tasty food. The food was easy to get. But in the country, he was safe from cats.

Moral

There's no such thing as a free meal.

In Other Words

Everything has a price. Better to work hard and live (and eat) in peace, than barely work at all and live in fear.

Reread the Fable

Analyze the Characters
- Who were the characters in this fable?
- How did the characters feel about their homes? Why?
- Who barely worked at all? What problem did this cause?
- Who had to work hard? What was his reward?

Analyze the Tools Writers Use
Idiom
Find examples of idioms in the fable.
- Did Town Mouse really want Country Mouse to hold a horse? What did Town Mouse mean? (page 8)
- Can someone's socks really come off because of food? What did Town Mouse mean? (page 8)
- On page 8, was Country Mouse really on a cloud? What did the author mean?
- On page 10, was Country Mouse really going to smack the road with his paw? What did he mean?

Focus on Words
Context Clues: Descriptions
Descriptions in a text can help readers figure out unfamiliar words. For example, Town Mouse and Country Mouse have very different opinions. The author describes an opinion as "different thoughts and ideas about the world." Reread the fable to find descriptions for the following story words.

Page	Word	Description	Meaning
7	superior		
7	determined		
8	delectable		
9	squeamish		

Belling the Cat

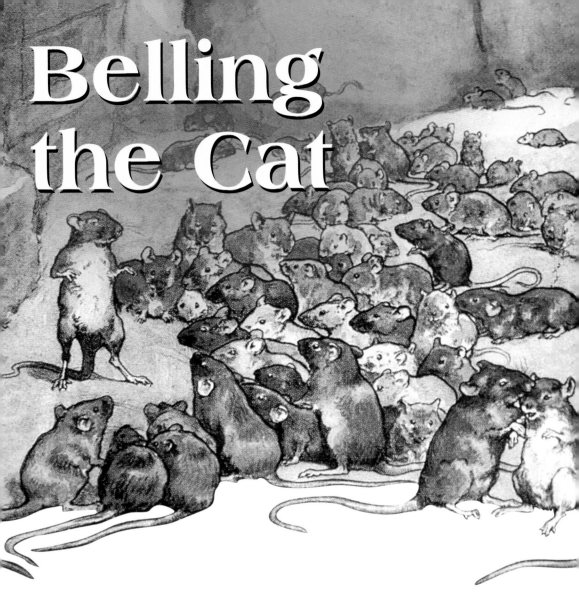

One nice day, the king of the mice got some **dreadful** news. His heart filled with doom and gloom. He got the house mice together. Then he broke the very bad news.

"We've got trouble," the old king said sadly. "The master of this house got a cat."

The mice looked at one another. They shrugged. They had never seen a cat before.

"What's so bad about a cat?" asked a baby mouse. "He could be my friend."

The old king sighed. "This cat doesn't want to be your friend. He will catch you. He will eat you."

"Oh!" cried the mice. "What should we do?"

"We can ask the cat to have dinner with us. We can make peace with him," said a young mouse.

The king sighed again. "If you ask a cat to have dinner with you, you will be the dinner. Cats have been chasing mice since the world began."

"We could write a sweet poem," said another mouse. "We could sing the cat's praises! We could tell of the cat's beauty. Would that help?"

"No, no, no," said the king.

"Then what should we do?" asked another mouse.

The king thought. "We must be all eyes and ears. If the cat is near, we must warn everyone."

One mouse ran to the front. He was a **sly** young mouse. He was clever. But he was also sneaky. He wanted to be the next king. "I have a plan," he said. "I will save all your lives."

"What is your plan, my child?" smiled the wise old king.

The sly mouse held up a bell. "We will put this bell around the neck of our **foe**. We will always hear our enemy the cat coming. Then we can run away."

"How will that be done?" asked the king.

"One of us will sneak up on the cat when he sleeps. He will quickly put the bell around his neck," said the clever mouse.

"Ah," said the old king, "except that cats have special powers. Even when their eyes are closed, they know you're coming."

"They do?"

"Oh yes. But you seem brave. Will you be the **courageous** mouse? Will you bell the cat? That would be a real feather in your cap. You would have something to brag about."

"Well, um," said the mouse, "I would love to. But I'm too busy!" Then he went back into the crowd. He bowed his head. He was quiet.

"That's what I thought," said the king.

Moral
Some things are easier said than done.

In Other Words
It is easy to say that something should be done, but much harder to actually do it.

Reread the Fable

Analyze the Characters
- Who were the characters in this fable?
- What big problem did the mice have?
- How did the sly mouse try to impress the other mice? What did they learn about him in the end?

Analyze the Tools Writers Use
Idiom
Find examples of idioms in the fable.
- On page 13: "Sing the cat's praises" really means . . .
- On page 13: "We must be all eyes and ears" really means . . .
- On page 14: "That would be a real feather in your cap" really means . . .

Focus on Words
Context Clues: Descriptions
Use descriptions in the text to help you figure out the meanings of unfamiliar words.

Page	Word	Description	Meaning
12	dreadful		
13	sly		
13	foe		
14	courageous		

The Dog and the Wolf

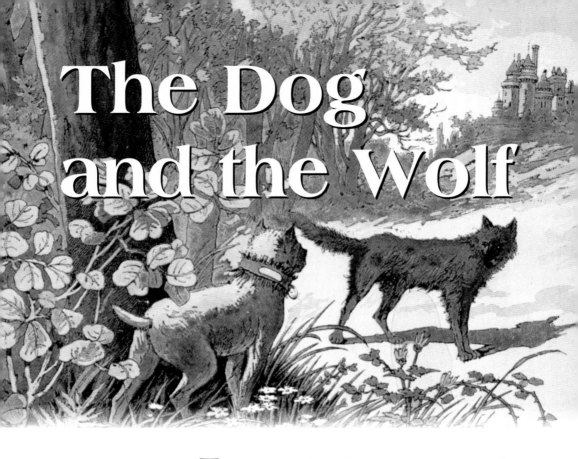

It was a hard winter. Every day was cold. The birds went south. They went to get warm. They went to find food. Many animals were **hibernating**. They slept in their burrows or caves during winter.

The author introduces one of the main characters, Wolf, by describing what he likes about the forest in the winter.

Wolf did not hibernate. He was wide awake. He went walking through the woods. Early in the winter, Wolf liked his long walks. He ran through the trees. He jumped in the snow. He did as he pleased. He had the whole forest to himself.

But then it got harder to find food. This winter had been the worst yet. Wolf had not eaten in days. He was very hungry.

One morning, Wolf saw a deer in the forest. Wolf tried to get the deer. But the deer was as quick as a wink. The deer got away.

The author introduces Wolf's problem. She shows how hard it is for Wolf to find or catch food.

Wolf was a sorry sight. He cried. He howled. Never before had a deer beaten him. And now he was very, very hungry.

"I will go to the river. I will catch fish," said Wolf to himself. "All I need to do is stand in the water. Maybe a fish will come to me."

Wolf slowly made his way to the river. He jumped in. *Splash!* The fish **darted** around him. They went swiftly this way and that way. Most of the fish swam away. Wolf got one tiny fish.

Many story events show how Wolf tries to solve his problem. Trying to catch fish is one way Wolf tries to solve his problem.

Wolf sat down by the river. He ate his one little fish. He wondered what he should do next.

Then Wolf heard barking. "That must be cousin Dog. I haven't seen him in ages," said Wolf. "I will call to him. Maybe he will help."

"Two shakes of a lamb's tail" is an idiom that means "quickly." The author could have said, "Dog was there quickly," but using the idiom makes the sentence more interesting. It also helps you form a picture in your mind.

Wolf used the last of his strength. He made a sad cry. "Oww! Oww!" Dog heard. He ran to Wolf. He was there in two shakes of a lamb's tail.

"Cousin Wolf, what is wrong?" asked Dog. "I heard your cry. You do not look well. You are as thin as a rail. Are you sick?"

"No," said Wolf. "But I am sick and tired of looking for food. That is all I do night and day."

"I can help you," said Dog. "Come and live with me on the farm. Work a little. You will get a lot of food. It's a great life."

"Will your master let me stay?" asked Wolf.

"My master has many chores. He needs someone to help," answered Dog. "I will tell him that you will work hard. You will work your tail off."

Wolf was happy. He was on top of the world. Now he would have a job. He would have food.

Dog told Wolf about his work. He helped his master hunt for wild **game**. Wolf could find any animal in the forest. "This will be a piece of cake for me," Wolf thought.

"Tell me, cousin Dog," Wolf said, "why is there no fur on your neck? Were you in a fight?"

"Oh, that is nothing," said Dog. "At night, my master puts a collar on me. He chains me up. It used to bother me. Now I am used to it. You will grow **accustomed** to it, too."

Wolf learns that Dog's life isn't perfect either. The author uses dialogue between the animals to show this. Notice that the author doesn't tell the reader what to think, but let's the reader decide based on what the characters say.

19

The author lets Wolf give the moral of the story.

"Oh no, cousin Dog," said Wolf. "I don't think I could ever be comfortable in chains. I will not grow used to it. I will never live that way. I was born to be free. I'd rather starve than be tied down."

Moral

It is better to die free than live in chains.

In Other Words

It is better to be free and starve than to be a well-fed slave.

Reread the Fable

Analyze the Characters
- Who were the characters in this fable?
- What was good about Dog's life? What was bad?
- What was good about Wolf's life? What was bad?
- Would you rather be Wolf or Dog? Why?

Analyze the Tools Writers Use
Idiom
Find examples of idioms in the fable.
- when Dog hurries quickly to Wolf's side (page 18)
- when Dog explains how he will introduce Wolf to the master (page 18)
- after Dog tells Wolf he can work for his master (page 18)
- when Wolf hears what type of work he would be doing for the master (page 18)

Focus on Words
Context Clues: Descriptions
Use descriptions in the text to help you figure out the meanings of unfamiliar words.

Page	Word	Description	Meaning
16	hibernating		
17	darted		
18	game		
19	accustomed		

How does an author write a

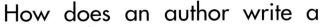

FABLE?

Reread "The Dog and the Wolf" and think about what the author did to write this fable. How did she develop the story? How can you, as a writer, develop your own fable?

1. Decide on a Moral

Remember that a fable teaches a lesson, or moral. In "The Dog and the Wolf," the author wanted to show that it is preferable to die free than to live in chains.

2. Brainstorm Characters

Writers ask these questions:
- What kind of animal is my main character?
- What human problem or flaw does my main character have?
- How does my main character show this problem or flaw? What does he or she do, say, or think?
- What other animal character will be important to my story? How will this character show that he or she does not have the same problem or flaw the main character has?

Character	Wolf	Dog
Traits	discouraged; willing to work for food	helpful; hardworking
Flaw/Asset	rather be free than be well-fed	rather be well-fed than free
Examples	He is good at the type of work the master needs, but he refuses the job because he doesn't want to be chained up.	He works hard and enjoys getting all the food he needs, but in return he is willing to be chained up.

 Brainstorm Setting and Plot
Writers ask these questions:
- Where does my fable take place? How will I describe it?
- What is the problem, or situation?
- What events happen?
- How does the fable end?

Setting	a forest in winter
Problem of the Story	Wolf cannot find enough food to eat.
Story Events	1. Wolf is starving. He is tired, weak, and miserable. He calls to his cousin Dog for help. 2. Dog says Wolf can come work with him at a farm. He could help the master hunt for wild game. 3. At first, Wolf is excited about the idea. Then he finds out he would have to be chained up at night.
Solution to the Problem	Wolf decides not to take the job. He would rather be free and find food another way.

Glossary

accustomed   (uh-KUS-tumd) adapted to existing conditions (page 19)

courageous   (kuh-RAY-jus) brave (page 14)

darted   (DAR-ted) moved suddenly or rapidly (page 17)

delectable   (dih-LEK-tuh-bul) delightful; pleasing to the taste (page 8)

determined   (dih-TER-mend) not giving up; driven to succeed (page 7)

dreadful   (DRED-ful) very bad (page 12)

foe   (FOH) an enemy (page 13)

game   (GAME) animals (such as deer or rabbits) that are hunted or taken in hunting (page 18)

hibernating   (HY-ber-nay-ting) sleeping or resting through the winter (page 16)

sly   (SLY) displaying cleverness (page 13)

squeamish   (SKWEE-mish) easily disgusted or repulsed (page 9)

superior   (soo-PEER-ee-er) of higher rank, quality, or importance (page 7)